ORCHARD BOOKS
338 Euston Road, London NW1 3BH
Orchard Books Australia
Level 17/207 Kent Street, Sydney, NSW 2000
First published in hardback in Great Britain in 2009 by Orchard Books
First published in paperback in 2010
ISBN 978 1 84616 753 9 (hardback)
ISBN 978 1 40830 777 9 (paperback)
Text © Michael Lawrence 2009
Illustrations © Tony Ross 2009
1 3 5 7 9 10 8 6 4 2 (hardback)
1 3 5 7 9 10 8 6 4 2 (paperback)
Printed in Great Britain
Orchard Books is a division of Hachette Children's Books,
an Hachette UK company.
www.hachette.co.uk

JACK FOUR'S JACKDAWS AND JACK of the GORGONS

MICHAEL LAWRENCE
TONY ROSS

ORCHARD BOOKS

JACK FOUR'S JACKDAWS

There were once four brothers named Jack. Their mother liked the name Jack. Her husband's name was Cyril.

Cyril Lovely was a farmer, and not a very good one, mainly because he preferred to spend his days in bed to farming, or shooting crows to farming, or doing anything you can think of to farming. Because of this the farm was in a very rundown condition, with nothing to eat but beetroot and bread. Occasionally they had a leg of pork, but the pig was on its last legs and they were saving those for Christmas.

'What are we going to do, Mother?' Cyril wailed one day.

'There's nothing for it,' his wife replied.

'One of the boys must go out into the world and seek his fortune and bring it home to share with the rest of us.'

So it was that the eldest Jack, Jack One, left the family hearth to seek his fortune, spotted handkerchief full of beetroot sandwiches on a stick over his shoulder, and the family sat down to wait for the money to roll in.

Three months passed and Jack One did not return.

'I reckon that boy's run off and spent his fortune,' Cyril Lovely said.

'Well then,' said Mrs Lovely, 'Jack Two must go and seek another. Jack,' she said to her second eldest, 'you make sure you come back now, and come back filthy rich, too, or you're for the high-jump.'

'Yes, Mum,' said Jack Two, and off he went to seek his fortune, beetroot sandwiches in a plain blue handkerchief on a stick over his shoulder, and the family sat down to wait for the money to roll in.

Three months went by and Jack Two had not returned.

'Well, there goes another fortune,' said Cyril. 'And I am so sick of bread and beetroot.'

'Jack,' said Mrs Lovely to her third eldest. 'Off with you and seek your fortune to stop us from starving like your good-for-nothing big brothers didn't.'

So Jack Three set off with his beetroot sandwiches in a striped handkerchief tied to a stick, and the family sat down to wait for the money to roll in.

But by the end of three months there was no sign of Jack Three and his fortune.

'Lads these days,' Cyril Lovely said. 'Out spending their fortunes and not a thought for their poor families back home. Well, nothing for it.' He jerked a thumb at Jack Four. 'Pack him a hanky, Ma.'

'Oh, not my baby,' Mrs Lovely cried, plunging the lad's face into her bosom, where he thrashed about trying not to suffocate.

'He's the only one left,' said Cyril. 'Not that I hold out much hope with him. Right little milksop, that one. Probably starve away from home.'

'He's starving at home,' Mrs Lovely reminded him. 'Wait,' she said then. 'I have an idea. Instead of his fortune, why don't we send him to find his brothers and tell them to come home at once and bring what's left of theirs?'

Cyril rather liked this wheeze, so Mrs Lovely made some beetroot sandwiches (with the crusts cut off), placed them in her best cotton hanky with lace trim, told young Jack to be careful crossing roads, and sat down with Cyril to wait while he set off to seek his brothers and their fortunes.

Now Jack Four had rarely been off the farm and knew too little of the world to be surprised when he came to an ivory tower, down which a mass of glorious golden locks cascaded. The locks – flowing from the head of a beautiful maiden leaning out of a tiny upper window – were being brushed by a maidservant on a ladder. Unlike her mistress the maidservant was not beautiful and if she complained more than she sang and scowled more than she smiled who can blame her, forced to brush someone else's hair every day of her rotten life?

'Pardon me,' said the youth, 'but I wonder if three young men called Jack have passed this way during the past nine months?'

At this the beautiful maiden up in the tower burst into tears and the servant jumped off her ladder in a fury. 'Now see what you done,' the maidservant said fiercely, and gave Jack a thwack with the hairbrush.

Jack reeled. 'But all I said was—'

'I knows full well what you said.' And the maidservant set about him good and proper, thwacking every part of him that he didn't manage to cover while lashing his poor bare ears with angry words.

'Jacks!' (Thwack)

'Promises, promises!'

(Thwack, thwack)

'Honeyed words and smooth talk!'

(Thwack) 'My poor mistress!'

(Thwack)

'"We'll go and seek our fortunes and come back and give you the earth!" they says to her.' (Thwack) 'And do they?' (Thwack) 'They do not!' (Thwack) 'Not hide nor hair nor brass front of any one of them has we seen since!' (Thwacketty-thwack) 'Be off with you or you'll get the back of my hand!'

'Girl!' the beautiful maiden cried from her lofty little window. 'Why have you stopped brushing? You know how tangled and lustreless my hair gets if it's not brushed continually. Proceed, no matter how upset I am.'

The servant climbed back up the ladder and resumed her task, and the dazed and battered Jack stumbled on his way.

Some hours later, having long polished off his beetroot sarnies and blown his nose on Mother's best hanky, Jack came upon a large kitchen garden whose vegetables seemed about to burst out of the ground in their eagerness to get into cooking pots. Beyond the garden was something even more interesting:

an orchard jammed with fruit of all kinds, fruit so large and luscious that he almost fainted with desire.

'I must have some of that fruit,' thought he, and fell to wondering how he might obtain it, for not a penny piece or cent or rouble or euro did he have on him. Nevertheless he unlatched the rather high garden gate and walked up the rather wide path to knock on the rather big door of the ramshackle shack at the heart of the glorious garden. After a thoroughly respectable pause heavy bolts were drawn back on the inside of the door.

Then the door creaked open a fat finger's

breadth and a large eye peered out.

'Sorry to bother you,' Jack said, 'but I'm hungry and I was wondering if—'

'Your name's not Jack, is it?' the deep voice interjected.

Jack started. 'Why yes it is, how did you know?'

'How did I know? Because the only people who come by these days are Jacks. The world seems to have been taken over by them. And what a lot of conniving crooks you are!'

The door slammed and the bolts bolted back.

Jack knew when he wasn't wanted, and he was about to leave when he caught sight of the orchard again, bulging with irresistible fruit. He knocked a second time.

'You still there?' growled the deep voice behind the door. 'Go away. You Jacks, you're all the same.'

'My dad doesn't think so,' Jack replied. 'He says I'm a milksop. He doesn't call any of the other Jacks that.'

'Milksop? He calls you that? That's what my dad used to call me.'

'You know what *it*'s like then,' said Jack.
'Fathers!'

The bolts were redrawn and the door again creaked open, though still only a fat finger's breadth. The large eye looked him up and down. Then down and up for a change.

'I only want a little piece of fruit,'
Jack said to the eye.

'I grow lovely fruit,' said the voice that
went with it. 'Veg too. My winter cabbage is
the best you ever saw, and the rabbits fight
over my carrots, and as for my turnips...'

'I'd rather have an apple,' said Jack.

'How about a pear?'

'Oh yes, two would go down very well.'

The door creaked open all the way, and in the doorway stooped the biggest, ugliest man Jack had never had nightmares about.

'An ogre!' he cried, falling back.

The ogre sighed. 'Sorry, I should have said. You don't have to come too near if I frighten you.'

'You don't f-f-f-frighten me,'

Jack stammered boldly.

'I don't like frightening people,' said the ogre. 'That's why my dad called me a milksop.'

Just then Jack noticed something else about the ogre. 'Your thumbs,' he said, dumping the stammer. 'They're green!'

The ogre raised his thumbs.

'The colour of growing things,' he said with pride. 'These thumbs can grow anything. Show me a hectare of barren land and in a single season I'll grow you a prize-winning garden.' He tucked his thumbs back into his enormous palms. 'Not that anyone ever gave me a prize. Well, why would they? Who am I? Just an ugly old ogre.'

He stepped out and led the way to the orchard, where he told Jack to help himself.

'Just don't do what those other Jacks did,' the ogre warned him.

'What did they do?'

'What did they do? I'll tell you what they did. They stole three of my most valued possessions, that's what.'

Jack was shocked. 'What were these possessions?'

'The first Jack took the monocle from my eye while I dozed after lunch,' the ogre told him. 'The second filched the narwhal-tusk nose-picker from my dressing table. And the third ran off with the solid gold eyebath from my medicine chest.'

'But that's shameful!' said Jack.

'It's what happens when you believe sob-stories about hunger and needing the toilet,' the ogre said sadly.

'I'll get your things back for you,' vowed Jack, packing fruit into his shirt like there was no tomorrow.

The ogre stared. 'Now why would you bother to do that?'

'To prove to you that all Jacks
aren't the same,' Jack said.
'As one milksop to another.'

That night Jack Four slept fitfully, plagued by indigestion from all the fruit he'd shoved into his face after leaving the ogre's. He had lain down by the side of the road, and when the sun rose next morning he tottered off, groaning, to continue his search for his brothers.

Some way along he came to a two-storey pebbledashed castle with neither a moat nor a drawbridge to put across it. A cart stood outside, a sleeping horse on its knees between the shafts. By the door there was a dangly bell and a notice. This is the notice:

SPELLS CAST
ALL TYPES
ENQUIRE WITHIN

(special rates for gullible nitwits)

'Maybe I can get a spell to ease my indigestion,' Jack thought, and yanked the dangly bell.

He waited. Nobody came. He pulled the bell a second time. Nobody came again. He lifted the latch.

The room he entered was plain and rather bare. On a desk lay some papers, two quill pens, a large globe of the world, a book of spells, and a magic wand. Jack picked up the wand, never having seen one before. As he turned it over in his hand, thinking how very ordinary it was, he noticed a glass display cabinet. The cabinet contained a variety of ornaments and keepsakes, including a magnifying glass, a small yellow walking stick, and a brass goblet.

'Skraaaaaaawk?'

Jack whirled about. On a table behind the door there stood a large cage in which three black birds – jackdaws – were jumping up and down fluttering their wings dementedly. He leaned towards the cage, frowning. There was something about the look in the birds' eyes and the cut of their feathers.

'Jack?' he said to the first jackdaw.

'Skraaaaaaaaaaaaaaaaaaaawk!' said the first jackdaw.

'Jack?' he said to the second jackdaw.

'Skraaaaaaaaaaaaaaaaaaaawk!' said the second jackdaw.

'Jack?' he said to the third jackdaw.

'Skraaaaaaaaaaaaaaaaaaaawk!' said the third jackdaw.

'My brothers!' said he to the three jackdaws, and 'SKRAAAWK!' said the three to him.

'What's all the noise?' another voice demanded. A small man, fresh from an early bath, ran in wearing nothing but a towel and an attractive selection of bubbles. 'First the doorbell half deafening me, then you lot making all this...'

Seeing Jack he skidded to a halt. Some of his bubbles popped.

'I didn't realise there was someone here,' he said. 'I'm not open till nine, you know. If you'd care to come back later I'm sure we can... Ah. I see you've been looking at my wand. Please put it down. A wizard's wand can be dangerous in the wrong hands.'

A PAIR OF JACKS

Jack had forgotten he was holding the wand. He looked at it. Then he looked at the wizard.

'Is this what turned my brothers into jackdaws?'

The wizard's towel slipped a notch. 'Your brothers?'

Jack indicated the cage, in which the jackdaws had fallen silent.

The wizard tightened his towel. 'Your brothers, were they? Well they got what was coming to them. They came to me one after the other seeking a cure for indigestion and when I'd cured them they informed me they couldn't pay my fee. So...'

'You turned them into jackdaws,' Jack said.

'I did. And I'm not ashamed of it. They deserve every rotten feather.'

Jack pointed the wand at the display cabinet. 'Did all that stuff belong to others who couldn't pay their bills, by any chance?'

'Don't wave that thing about!' shrieked the wizard.

Too late. The display cabinet was already turning into a giant scarab beetle with a cracked bedpan on its back. In the pan were all the things from the cabinet. 'Oops,' said Jack.

'I liked that cabinet,' the wizard said sadly.

'Well you can change it back, can't you?'

'No. That wand's getting on a bit, its magic is almost done. Still casts mild spells but it's not much good for uncasting any more.'

'So get yourself a new one,' Jack suggested.

50 Quid

'Would that I could, but trade isn't what it was. Everyone wants something for nothing and new wands aren't cheap.'

'Does that mean that you can't change my brothers back either?'

'That's about the size of it,' said the wizard.

Jack scratched his head.

Scratching his head always helped him think, though it didn't do much for his dandruff. Unfortunately, his scratching hand held a magic wand today, and as he scratched it twiddled in the wizard's direction. The wizard threw up his hands in horror and the towel said hello to his feet.

'Don't wave it about, I said, don't wave it ab... Oh dear. Oh dear, oh dear,

oh...

Croak.'

The croak came from the large soapy toad in the middle of the big white towel on the floor.

'Sorry,' said Jack, and returned the wand carefully to the desk. As he did so, he realised that his indigestion had gone.

Later that same day …

Jack Four hauled at the reins. The wizard's horse came to a halt, and the cart with it. He jumped down, opened the gate, strode up the path, and knocked on the door. Heavy bolts were drawn back, the door opened a fat finger's breadth, and a large eye appeared in the gap.

'Wot?'

'It's me, Jack the milksop. I've brought back the things that were stolen from you by the other Jacks.'

A sharp intake of ogre breath. 'You've brought my things back? You've actually brought them back like you promised?'

Jack opened a carrier bag and displayed the three items which had caught his eye in the display cabinet before it became a bedpan: the magnifying glass, the small yellow stick, and the brass goblet. 'One monocle,' he said, 'one narwhal-tusk nose-picker, one solid gold eyebath, returned to their rightful owner.'

The eye in the gap grew moist. 'I don't know what to say,' the ogre said, which shows that this wasn't quite true. 'No one's ever been kind to me before. So there are good Jacks in the world. Well, one. For this act of kindness I'll be your devoted servant for life. I'll follow you wherever you go.'

'That's really not necessary,' said Jack.

'No, I insist,' said the ogre. 'Where are we off to, O master?'

'I'm taking my brothers home.'

The ogre looked about him. 'I see no brothers.'

Jack led him up the garden path, through the gate, and showed him the cage on the cart, and the three jackdaws within it.

'I see,' said the ogre, more interested in the small head that was suddenly poking out of Jack's pocket. 'What's that you have there, O Mightiest of Milksops?'

'Ah, just a toad.'
Jack said, taking the
toad from his pocket.
'I'm very fond of
toads,' the ogre said.

Jack held out his open palm, on which the toad now sat. 'He's all yours.'

The ogre took the toad. 'Coochie-coo,' he said, and bunged it in his mouth. He crunched hard. A green leg kicked once between his lips, then fell limp as old asparagus. 'That was wizard,' the ogre said as the toad croaked.

They set off,

Jack riding the horse that
pulled the cart,

the ogre lumbering behind

picking tiny bones out of his gums.

Before long they reached the ivory tower where the beautiful maiden still leaned out of her high window while her bad-tempered servant brushed her golden locks from a ladder.

'You again!' the maidservant cried. 'And who's your ugly friend?'

'He's an ogre,' said Jack Four.

'Sorry about that,' said the ogre.

'I have something for your mistress.' Jack said, jumping down from the cart and holding up the globe of the world from the wizard's desk.

'Eh?' said the maidservant.

'The first three Jacks promised her the earth, you said. Well I've brought it for her, on their behalf. Best I could do, I'm afraid.'

The maidservant laughed – a very rare event – and slid down the ladder. 'Look, mistress!' she called up to the high window. 'This likely lad has brought you the earth! Not quite what we hoped for, but you have to see the funny side!'

Her mistress did not.

'I expected a kingdom! Great riches! Pretty golden slippers! Whipped cream doughnuts! Oh-oh, sob-sob, what a life! Get back on the ladder, girl, and brush my hair while I do my sorry best to come to terms with my misfortune.'

But the maidservant did not get back on the ladder and brush her hair. She hurled the brush to the ground and kicked the ladder away.

'Brush it yourself!' she said. 'Nothing pleases you, does it? Moan, moan, moan all day long. Never done a day's work in your life and never happy for a minute. Well, I've had it with you!' She turned to Jack. 'Youth, you have a good heart and good hearts are rare these days. I'm coming with you, and if you're not attached I'll do you the honour of giving you my hand, what do you say to that?'

'Your hand?' said Jack, eyeing it with suspicion.

'It's settled then.'
The ex-maidservant
   climbed up on the cart.
'Drive on,
   hubby-to-be!'

As they drove away they heard the wailings and beseechings of the blubbing maiden in the high window. 'Don't leave me, don't go, who'll brush my glorious golden locks, who, who, who, oh what shall I do?'

'You can find another skivvy, that's what you can do!' her former maid yelled back, gripping Jack's arm and snuggling close.

The first thing Jack Four saw when they reached the farm was his father shooting crows up in the top field. The second thing was his mother rushing out to greet him. Jack introduced his fiancé and the ogre. Mrs Lovely whispered that she liked the look of the ogre but she wasn't so sure about the one with the bad hair, bad teeth and bad attitude. Then she demanded to know why Jack had come home without his brothers. He showed her the cage on the back of the cart.

'Here they are, Mother.

Jack,

Jack

and Jack,

home again safe
and sound, if
a bit beaky.'

Mrs Lovely gawped at the birds.

'What are you talking about, boy?'

'They were turned into jackdaws by a wizard,' he explained. 'Unfortunately he got to them before they could find their fortunes, but isn't it good to have them home again?'

His mother shook her head sadly. 'Oh Jack, you'd believe anything. My great hulking boys turned into jackdaws? Really!'

And she flung back the door of the cage and threw the birds into the air. After being cooped up for so long they spread their wings and flew high, swooping and diving and tumbling with pleasure, intending to return shortly to help their little brother convince their mother that they were indeed her long lost sons.

Up in the top field Cyril Lovely saw them. 'Rotten birds!' he growled. 'No matter what you does, they still keeps a-comin'.'

He raised his gun once more, and—

CRACK!

CRACK!

CRACK!

—the spinning, tumbling jackdaws, turning back into three large youths – large dead youths – plummeted from the sky and—

THUD!

THUD!

THUD!

—landed one after the other on their father, squashing him to beetroot.

After the four funerals, life soon settled down at the farm. Jack married the ex-maid, who thwacked him for nothing all the time, Mrs Lovely proposed to the ogre, who told her to get on her bike – he was more interested in turning the barren land into a rainforest – and years passed, as they tend to do if you wait long enough.

One day Jack (now promoted to Jack One) was out walking with his three sons (all called Jack) when they came upon an ivory tower, from a high window of which leaned a clean white skeleton. Amazingly, the skeleton still had all its hair, a great hanging mass of it, tangled and dull and ribboned with ivy. Jack considered putting the ladder up against the tower and snipping off the hair to take back to his wife as a keepsake, but he knew that she would only thwack him for his trouble so he decided not to bother. He looked along the road. A whole world lay at the end of it and he'd seen less than a thimbleful.

'What do you say we go seek our fortune, lads?' he said to his three sons.

'Cool with us, Pop,' said the new

Jack Two,

Jack Three and

Jack Four.

And that's what they did. They found one too. A truly fantastic fortune. The kind of fortune adventurers only dream about, which made them rich beyond the dreams of Avarice (whoever he was). And did they go straight back home with it?

Don't make me laugh.

A PAIR OF JACKS

JACK of the GORGONS

Jack Cheesefeet was called Jack Cheesefeet not because he was the cheesemaker's son (which he was) but because he never – I mean **never** – changed his socks. Jack's socks were disgusting. His father said they smelt like the worst cheese in the world, and he knew a thing or two about cheese, did Jack's dad.

Well this story is about what happened when Jack Cheesefeet met some gorgons.

Gorgons, in case you don't know, are terrifying female creatures with great writhing, twisting snakes for hair. They do lots of really nasty things, like let their noses run and run, and spit all over the place when they speak. But the worst thing of all is this. When a human meets a gorgon's eye, that human is instantly turned to stone.

Yes, really.

Now one fine May morning two of these unpleasant types entered the village in northern Italy where Jack and his father lived. One of the gorgons was called Gawful and the other was called Greadful, and as they slurthered along the main street the villagers came out to stare at them.

And were instantly turned to stone.

The two gorgons whooped with delight and danced around the stone villagers, taunting them and tipping rubbish over them and writing rude words on their foreheads. Then they took up residence in two tall wooden towers at opposite ends of the village and fell into a deep and dreamless gorgonsleep while the poor villagers remained outside their homes, as still and cold as garden gnomes, but bigger.

There was only one villager who was not turned to stone, and that was young Jack, who'd been off fishing for tiddlers since the crack of eight to get out of helping his father make cheese. Heading homeward around noon and approaching the village, a wax-curdling sound met Jack's ears. He skidded to a horrified halt. He knew gorgon snores when he heard them. Without ado, he threw his sack of tiddlers in the air and himself on a prickly thorn bush.

'Yaaaaaaaaaagggggggh!'

he cried

(because thorns are painful).

On hearing Jack's 'Yaaaaaaaaaggggggh!' Gawful and Greadful jerked awake. Their scrawny necks swivelled and the snakes on their scalps writhed and hissed. 'VOT VOZ ZAT?!' the gorgons screeched in that interesting accent of theirs.

And then they spied Jack prising himself carefully off the thorn bush. Leaping from their towers, they loped towards him on their strergly legs, snarling nastily and flinging great gollups of gorgonspit in all directions at once.

Jack, of course, ran for his life, and might even have escaped the gorgons' clutches if he hadn't done the most brain-swerglingly stupid thing that any Jack has ever done.

He looked over his shoulder.

He met their eyes.

And was instantly turned to stone.

Bad news for Jack, bad news indeed, but others soon had cause to celebrate, for the one thing that can break the gorgonspell that turns people to stone is fresh warm gorgonspit, the very stuff that Gawful and Greadful, going after Jack, had spattered so carelessly over everything – including the stone villagers, who...

Twitched.
Yawned.
Stretched.
Scratched.
Spake.

'Fellow villagers!' boomed the Mayor. 'Let us pursue and slay those villainous fiends!'

And the villagers reached for their gorgon-gartering gear and set off after Gawful and Greadful, who were so busy congratulating themselves on having turned yet another human to stone that they didn't see their pursuers until they were almost on their hideous heels. But then they turned and glared with their horrible eyes.

The villagers halted at once, causing a lot of them to bump into another lot of them, but the gorgons continued to glare, keen to turn them back into stone even though they'd stopped. And what do you think happened? I'll tell you.

Nothing.

Not one of the villagers was returned to stone.

'It's true!' said Tom the taxidermist.

'What is?' said Watt the whittler.

'The old tale,' said Tom.

'What old tale?' said Watt. (He wasn't called Watt for nothing.)

'The urban legend that once you've been turned to stone by a gorgon and the spell's been broken by gorgonspit you can never be turned to stone again. Not by a gorgon anyway!'

Now that they knew this, the villagers threw themselves on the two monsters. They showed them no mercy – not a bit or drop of it – tearing them grerp from grerp and gruttle from gruttle. They even cut their gnerkers off.

Jack Cheesefeet was now the only stoned villager, but Gawful and Greadful were no longer in a position to spit at him and return him to his former flesh-and-blood self, so the others, though dripping with gorgonyuk, carried him back to the village, singing as they marched. They were very grateful to Jack. If he hadn't woken the gorgons and made them spit so furiously, they would still be standing outside their homes doing bad garden gnome impressions.

The villagers built a plinth in the village square near the cheese shop and placed Jack upon it like a statue. The butcher's apprentice suggested they call him Plinth Jack, but someone gave him a thick ear for his trouble. Words were chiselled on Jack's stone plinth by the village chiseller.

JACK OF THE GORGONS
HERO

The villagers did one other thing besides.
They gave the village a new name.
Gorgonzola.

Now the tale of what happened that day in Gorgonzola spread like gorgonspit, and in no time a new legend sprang up. This one claimed that Jack had single-handedly slain fifty gorgons with his bare hands, made footballs of their heads, hockey sticks of their legs, and vases of their bottoms. It wasn't a bad legend as legends go, but the one thing it failed to mention was that Jack had been turned to stone and that stone he remained. Because the legend overlooked this tiny detail, it was generally assumed that he still went gorgon hunting when the mood was upon him.

Not a bad thing really because, quaking with fear of this mighty human, the gorgons of the region packed their spittoons and moved to Switzerland to invent clocks.

There was just one gorgon who was not scared off by the legend of Jack of the Gorgons, and her name was Gobnoxious. Gobnoxious was beside herself with fury at what this Jack was said to have done to her kind, and vowed to get even with him if it took every last strerg in her body.

Now it's possible that there has never, in the entire history of gorgonkind, been a gorgon quite as hideous and bad-tempered as Gobnoxious. Taller and stringier than most gorgons, she had more snakes on her head than any other and more spit in her than at least half a dozen. Her eyes were like black olives, her lips like frayed rope, and her teeth bore more than a passing resemblance to chewed pencil stubs. She certainly wasn't the kind of person you'd welcome with open arms when she turned up in your village at 2.15 on a sunny September afternoon.

'Vhere is zis Jack?' Gobnoxious shrieked as she slurthered into Gorgonzola at the 2.15 in question. 'I veel rrrip him apart and feed his rrremains to ze crows, and zen I'll sink of somesing unpleasant to do to him!'

No one answered. Not a pin could be heard dropping. The villagers had all run into their houses and bolted their doors and slammed their shutters and stuffed their lodgers up the chimney. The only villager still about was stone Jack on his plinth outside the cheese shop, and the monstrous gorgon had no idea he was not a statue. He looked like one, with geraniums growing in his pockets, the calling cards of passing pigeons dribbling down his face, and memos like 'Must remember the broccoli' on some of his more private parts. But statue or not, when Gobnoxious read

JACK OF THE GORGONS

HERO

…the snakes on her head hissed themselves into a frenzy and she raised her gnarled old gorgonclub and brought it down upon stoned Jack with all her mighty might.

'Take thet, yer mizzerable jerrk!' she snerrked. 'And thet, yer creepy little berrk!' she struck again and again and again and with every blow a gollup of bubbly gorgonspit flew from her abominable gob, so that in no time Jack was fairly dripping.

And you know what **that** means.

His fingers twitched.

He blinked.

His disgusting socks began to steam.

Realising at last that the statue was not a statue, but her sworn enemy in person, Gobnoxious drew herself up to her full height and prepared to fling herself upon him and do her worst.

But then the smell of Jack's socks hit her.

Her nostrils flared in gorgonish horror.

She reeled.

She staggered.

She clutched her grerps.

Oh no! Not cheese!
Anything but cheese!

Gorgons, you see, are allergic to cheese. Horribly allergic. When a gorgon smells really strong cheese (or anything as devastatingly similar to it as Jack's socks) unfortunate things happen to them.

Their eyes shoot out on crusty stalks and catch fire.

Their filthy teeth crack.

Their lips flake off.

They swell up in unfortunate places.

The snakes on their heads writhe out of control and throttle one another.

In fact, all in all, they get pretty cheesed off.

These things now happened to Gobnoxious. Spitting and spewing like an overfull kettle on the boil, she backed away from Jack and bumped into the great open vat of new cheese his father had been skimming of dead flies before her arrival. Into the vat she tumbled, and, thrashing wildly, sank to the bottom in agony, coming apart at the gorgonseams as she went.

Then, apart from the odd little fart of rising bubbles, there was silence. The villagers savoured the silence. It was good. Cautiously, they summoned the courage to open their shutters and doors and peek outside.

And what a sight met their eyes!

There was Jack of the Gorgons, flesh and blood once more (though still covered with pigeon droppings and other personal messages) staring into the vat of cheese with bewilderment. The villagers came out and gathered round the vat, gulping at the bits of cheesy gorgon jerking to the surface.

'He's done it again!' they murmured in awe. 'Young Jack's defeated the gorgon menace yet **again**!'

They pounded Jack on the back and danced round and round him trying not to notice the stink of his socks, and for a second time Jack Cheesefeet was the hero of the hour.

I believe it was the postmaster who leant over the vat and poked a finger in one of the bulging bloodshot eyes bobbing about on top. Lifting his finger (covered in cheese-and-gorgon mix) he plunged it into his mouth, then fell straight to the ground, quivering from neck to knee.

The villagers thought this a huge joke and when the gorgon-flavoured cheese was set they sliced off chunks of it to send to relatives who always forgot their birthdays. By the time it arrived at its various destinations the cheese ponged so badly that the recipients had to find pegs for their noses to stop their nostrils healing up. And when they tasted the cheese they too fell straight to the ground quivering from neck to knee – and promptly sent to Gorgonzola for more to send to other miserable devils.

Orders were soon coming from far and wide. The new cheese was in such demand that the vat of grumpled gorgon grap was soon empty.

Ordinarily, Jack's cheesemaker father might have tried to make something similar because it was so popular, but he'd had enough of all these gorgons slurthering into his village whenever they felt like it and taken the Tuesday cart to Parma to start a new business, producing a cheese called Parmesan, and a variety of ham to go with it in sandwiches.

With his father gone Jack, like it or not, was Master Cheesemaker of Gorgonzola, and it fell to him to fulfil the orders for the new cheese. But this was not easily done. The cheese required a certain vital ingredient and you couldn't just stroll into the corner shop and ask for six slices of gorgonwurst or a kilo of gorgonknerkers. It didn't even come in tins.

But then Jack had
the one brilliant idea of his life.

He took all his foulest, smelliest, uncleanest socks and waggled them in milk that had gone off, and when the milk set hard it was so like the terrible cheese that everyone who sampled it fell straight to the ground quivering from neck to knee.

So Jack Cheesefeet's fortune was made.

Now all this happened a very long time ago, and sadly, no one honours Jack of the Gorgons today. Gorgonzola Cheese, however, is famous the world over, though the main ingredient (Essence of Gorgon) is supplied by a small company in Poland that makes stink bombs for joke shops. Its formula is a closely guarded secret. If you are tempted to try the famous cheese for yourself, you might spare a thought for the Jack who gave it to the world as you fall straight to the ground quivering from neck to knee.

I'm sure he'd like to be remembered for something other than his stinking socks.

A PAIR OF JACKS

JACK and the GIANT-KILLER
AND JACKWITCH   978 1 40830 774 8

JACK
AND F

JACK
AND

JACK
AND